# YOU CALL THE PLAY:

# BASEBALL

# Catcher in Command

## BY PETER STRUPP

*A Sports Illustrated For Kids Book*

BANTAM BOOKS

TORONTO • NEW YORK • LONDON • SYDNEY • AUCKLAND

You Call the Play: Baseball
Catcher in Command
A Bantam Book/April 1994

Cover and interior design by Miriam Dustin
Illustrations by Daryl Cagle

For information address: Bantam Books

ISBN 0-553-48161-4

Published simultaneously in the United States and Canada

Bantam Books are published by Bantam Books, a division of Bantam
Doubleday Dell Publishing Group, Inc. Its trademark, consisting of the
words "Bantam Books" and the portrayal of a rooster, is Registered in U.S.
Patent and Trademark Office and in other countries. Marca Registrada.
Bantam Books, 1540 Broadway, New York, New York, 10036.

PRINTED IN THE UNITED STATES OF AMERICA

CWO 0 9 8 7 6 5 4 3 2 1

YOU CALL THE PLAY: BASEBALL is more than a baseball book you read. It is a baseball *game* book you can play! And as the Kid, a rookie catcher called up from the minor leagues, you're in for the game of your life. When your manager and starting catcher are suddenly sidelined, it's up to you to manage your team from behind the plate.

You won't read this book straight through as you would a normal story. Instead you'll come face-to-face with some tough baseball situations and be given a choice of which play you want to call. After you choose, follow the instructions at the bottom of the page to find out if your strategy worked. Two announcers will tell you what happens on the field.

Each decision you make will lead to a new situation and will eventually affect the outcome of the game. You may win big or head back to the clubhouse in defeat. But best of all, 30 different game endings let you play and replay the action — and it's a whole new ball game every time.

Now tuck in your shirt and look alive out there.

**THE PLACE:** Metropolitan Park, the Blue Sox home field. Built in 1925 in the middle of the city, Metropolitan Park is a natural-grass, baseball-only park with a short (310') rightfield fence that makes it a lefty-slugger's paradise.

**THE GAME:** Blue Sox vs. Barons, in the first game after the All-Star break — about midway through the season. The Barons lead the Blue Sox by 2½ games in the race for the division pennant.

# R O S T E R S

## BLUE SOX (This is your team, Kid.)

**Grampa Graff, manager.** Grampa is considered one of baseball's greatest teachers. The Blue Sox front office sometimes sends him to the minors for a season to manage talented youngsters. That's where you, the Kid, met Grampa. Grampa's getting pretty old, though, and he can get distracted during games. His coaches are Grumpy Sternemann at first base and Ron Cron at third.

### THE LINEUP

| Order | Player | Pos. | Bats | Average | HRs | RBIs | SBs |
|---|---|---|---|---|---|---|---|
| 1 | **Harold Carlson** | LF | R | .368 | 6 | 28 | 28 |

Harold could win the batting title *and* the stolen-base crown.

| | | | | | | | |
|---|---|---|---|---|---|---|---|
| 2 | **Speedy Green** | SS | R | .320 | 2 | 31 | 19 |

Speedy is a reliable hitter and a blur on the base paths.

| | | | | | | | |
|---|---|---|---|---|---|---|---|
| 3 | **Denny Hill** | 1B | L | .297 | 13 | 42 | 2 |

Denny can hit for both power and average. At age 35, he is the oldest player on the team — and the slowest runner.

| | | | | | | | |
|---|---|---|---|---|---|---|---|
| 4 | **Stroke Thurman** | RF | L | .210 | 20 | 62 | 3 |

Just 23 years old, Stroke is in the chase for the home-run crown. He is a lefthanded pull hitter, which means he usually hits the ball to rightfield.

| | | | | | | | |
|---|---|---|---|---|---|---|---|
| 5 | **Rusty Mills** | CF | L | .250 | 12 | 45 | 7 |

Rusty is a solid all-around player. He is also a pull hitter.

| | | | | | | | |
|---|---|---|---|---|---|---|---|
| 6 | **Cal Scott** | C | L | .302 | 10 | 35 | 0 |

Cal is an 11-year veteran. You, the Kid, were brought up to learn from him and to replace him eventually. Cal is a pull hitter and a slow base runner.

| Order | Player | Pos. | Bats | Average | HRs | RBIs | SBs |
|---|---|---|---|---|---|---|---|
| 7 | **Hector Peña** | 2B | R | .280 | 2 | 20 | 13 |

Hector is a solid hitter with good speed but not much power.

| 8 | **Kevin Finley** | 3B | R | .268 | 3 | 26 | 9 |
|---|---|---|---|---|---|---|---|

A streaky second-year player, Kevin is in a batting slump.

| | **Team** | | 4R, 4L | **.267** | **68** | **299** | **81** |
|---|---|---|---|---|---|---|---|

## THE BENCH

| Player | Pos. | Bats | Average | HRs | RBIs | SBs |
|---|---|---|---|---|---|---|
| **The Kid** | C | R | .315 | 3 | 9 | 2 |

This is you. The front office brought you up from the minors three weeks ago. You're new to the big leagues and opposing pitchers don't know your strengths or weaknesses. Your catching skills are excellent, but catcher is a position where experience also counts.

| **Mike Gilmore** | OF | L | .288 | 9 | 24 | 0 |
|---|---|---|---|---|---|---|

You could wake Mike in the middle of the night, hand him a bat, and he'd get a hit. A reliable pinch-hitter.

## THE PITCHING STAFF

| Pitcher | Throws | W-L | ERA | Innings | Ks | BBs | Saves |
|---|---|---|---|---|---|---|---|
| **Hub King** | L | 10-3 | 2.93 | 100.2 | 90 | 50 | — |

Hub is a starter with a great fastball and a decent off-speed pitch. He can be wild early.

| **Ed Neighbor** | R | 9-2 | 3.24 | 87.0 | 70 | 32 | — |
|---|---|---|---|---|---|---|---|

Ed is also a starter. He was once a fastballer, but he hurt his shoulder. Now he relies on curveballs, change-ups, and control.

| **Ron Richter** | R | 4-3 | 4.43 | 35.0 | 32 | 15 | 10 |
|---|---|---|---|---|---|---|---|

Ron is a veteran long reliever with good control. He throws mostly curves and off-speed pitches.

| **Alan Sorensen** | R | 1-0 | 4.23 | 20.0 | 20 | 11 | 14 |
|---|---|---|---|---|---|---|---|

A fastballer with a great arm but no endurance, Alan is one of two Blue Sox closers. They pitch in relief late in close games.

| **Ned Kelly** | L | 1-1 | 3.57 | 25.0 | 23 | 11 | 20 |
|---|---|---|---|---|---|---|---|

The team's southpaw closer, Ned is a clever veteran with a wide variety of pitches and great control.

## BARONS (This is your opponent.)

**Buddy Phipps, manager.** Buddy struts like a peacock, and his team swaggers along behind him. Buddy has called the Blue Sox "that bunch of wimps," and he has predicted the Barons will win the pennant by at least 10 games.

## THE LINEUP

| Order | Player | Pos. | Bats | Average | HRs | RBIs | SBs |
|---|---|---|---|---|---|---|---|
| 1 | **Lonnie Snyder** | LF | R | .334 | 9 | 29 | 16 |

The most dangerous leadoff batter in the league, Snyder can hit for average and for power, and he can steal bases.

| | | | | | | | |
|---|---|---|---|---|---|---|---|
| 2 | **J.R. James** | 2B | R | .328 | 8 | 26 | 14 |

His initials should be TNT — because he is so explosive.

| | | | | | | | |
|---|---|---|---|---|---|---|---|
| 3 | **Buzz Saw Bradshaw** | C | R | .280 | 14 | 45 | 2 |

A pull hitter with good power, Bradshaw is an on-field version of his manager. He is very slow on the bases.

| | | | | | | | |
|---|---|---|---|---|---|---|---|
| 4 | **Walt Metcalf** | 1B | L | .208 | 24 | 66 | 0 |

Metcalf is leading the home-run race. He is also a pull hitter and a slow, slow base runner.

| | | | | | | | |
|---|---|---|---|---|---|---|---|
| 5 | **Ace Edwards** | RF | L | .275 | 17 | 50 | 5 |

Edwards is another pull hitter, and he is a great all-around player.

| | | | | | | | |
|---|---|---|---|---|---|---|---|
| 6 | **Herm Davis** | CF | R | .262 | 10 | 38 | 10 |

Davis has a fast bat, fast feet, and a quick temper.

| | | | | | | | |
|---|---|---|---|---|---|---|---|
| 7 | **Vince Rizzo** | SS | R | .240 | 10 | 33 | 4 |

Rizzo rounds out the Barons' "Home Run Row."

| | | | | | | | |
|---|---|---|---|---|---|---|---|
| 8 | **Rodney Hammond** | 3B | R | .180 | 6 | 20 | 1 |

A struggling rookie, Hammond can hit the ball a mile — when he connects.

| | | | | | | | |
|---|---|---|---|---|---|---|---|
| **Team** | | | 6R, 2L | **.246** | **98** | **316** | **52** |

## THE PITCHER

| | Throws | W-L | ERA | Innings | Ks | BBs | Saves |
|---|---|---|---|---|---|---|---|
| **Ken Rhodes** | L | 9-3 | 3.16 | 106.0 | 83 | 28 | — |

Rhodes leads the majors with 10 complete games. He has a great fastball and great control.

# PLAY BALL!

7

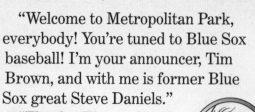

"Welcome to Metropolitan Park, everybody! You're tuned to Blue Sox baseball! I'm your announcer, Tim Brown, and with me is former Blue Sox great Steve Daniels."

"Thanks, Tim, and hello everybody. Today, in our first game after the All-Star break, we have the makings of a real barn-burner: two strong clubs, neck and neck in a pennant race, but about as different as they can be. The Blue Sox have the lightning and the Barons have the thunder."

"That's right, Steve. Our Blue Sox are leading the league in batting *and* stolen bases. Meanwhile, the Barons have six players with a chance to hit 20 or more home runs this season. Speaking of hitting, what do you think of the Blue Sox' new rookie?"

"I like the looks of the Kid, Tim. The Kid's a smart batter and solid behind the plate. By the way, where is the Kid?"

"The Kid isn't starting today, Steve. And I'm beginning to wonder who Grampa Graff is starting on the mound. The Barons will go with Ken Rhodes, but Grampa hasn't named the Blue Sox starting pitcher yet. C'mon, Grampa! Who'll it be?"

Inning: 1    At Bat: Barons
Score: Barons 0, Blue Sox 0

Ed Neighbor (R) 9-2, 3.24 ERA *or*
Hub King (L) 10-3, 2.93 ERA

"Hey, Kid! Come over here!"
Grampa Graff is calling you.

"I'm feeling poorly, Kid. I must've eaten some bad clams. I'm going to need a little help managing the team. I can't decide between Hub King and Ed Neighbor as our starter. What do *you* think?"

**THE KID**

Let's see, what are the things to consider in picking a starting pitcher? It's usually harder for a lefthanded batter to hit pitches thrown by a lefthanded pitcher and for a righthanded batter to hit against a righthanded pitcher. Do the Barons have more righties or lefties?

Also, home-run-hitting teams usually are good fastball hitters, while teams with high batting averages do better against a pitcher who throws a variety of pitches. What kind of team are the Barons? What kind of pitchers are Hub and Ed?

- To start Ed Neighbor, turn to page 10.
- To start Hub King, turn to page 62.

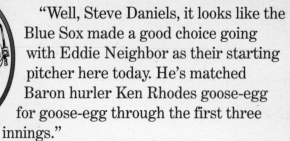

"Well, Steve Daniels, it looks like the Blue Sox made a good choice going with Eddie Neighbor as their starting pitcher here today. He's matched Baron hurler Ken Rhodes goose-egg for goose-egg through the first three innings."

"You got that right, Tim. I don't think the Barons could hit Eddie if they were swinging surfboards. His variety of pitches is keeping them guessing and his control is about as good as you could hope for. He's just been picking at the corners of the strike zone. Now let's see what he can do with a bat."

"The Blue Sox are at bat in the bottom of the third with no score. Hector Peña is on first with a single. The second batter, Kevin Finley, flied out to right. So, with one out, Blue Sox pitcher Ed Neighbor is stepping up to the plate. Let's see if the home team tries something tricky to move the runner into scoring position."

| Batter | Balls | Strikes | Outs |
|--------|-------|---------|------|
| Neighbor, P | 0 | 0 | 1 |

"For corn sakes, Kid, our pitcher's up and he's facing one of the best hurlers in the game! I don't know what we should do. One thing I do know is I'm not ordering those clams again." Grampa rolls over, groaning. That leaves you to make the call.

Let's see, Ed's batting .102. If he hits the ball, he'd most likely swing late and hit it to rightfield. If it falls in for a single, it could put Hector on third with one out. If it's caught, we'll have a runner on first with two outs.

On the other hand, Ed spends a lot of time working on his bunting. A good bunt will move Hector to second and give Harold Carlson, your best hitter, a chance to drive him home.

- To have Ed swing away, turn to page 28.
- To have Ed bunt, turn to page 12.

11

"Rhodes sets and delivers. It's a bunt! Catcher Buzz Saw Bradshaw scoops it up and fires to first for the out. Hector Peña moves to second on the sacrifice. Steve?"

"That was a good call, Tim. It brings up Harold Carlson with a runner in scoring position."

"Harold digs in at the plate, Steve. A ball . . . a strike . . . and a hard smash up the middle for a single! Hector rounds third and scores easily. Speedy Green is the next batter, and he punches the first pitch down the rightfield line for an extra-base hit. Harold scores from first, and Speedy cruises into second with a double. Stroke Thurman hits a long fly ball that's caught at the warning track for the third out. But, after three innings, the Blue Sox lead 2-0."

*Neither team scores in the fourth or fifth innings.*

"The Barons are cooking up some trouble here in the top of the sixth, Steve. Lonnie Snyder is on second and J. R. James is on first with two outs. Ace Edwards is batting with a 2-2 count."

"Look, Tim! Catcher Cal Scott is bent over coughing. Now he's running into the dugout. I wonder what's up."

12

| Inning: 6 | At Bat: Barons |
| :-- | :-- |
| Score: Blue Sox 2, Barons 0 | |

| Batter | Balls | Strikes | Outs |
| :-- | :-- | :-- | :-- |
| Edwards, RF | 2 | 2 | 2 |

What happened? Grampa will tell you.

"Cal must have swallowed his chewing tobacco. I'd be surprised if he doesn't have to go to the hospital. You're in, Kid. I'll signal if I have any plays to call. Otherwise, you're on your own."

**THE KID**

Okay, you're behind the plate: Two outs, fast runners on base, and Edwards up with a 2-2 count. Maybe the Barons will try the hit-and-run and have the runners going on the pitch to see if they can both score on a base hit. If you call for a pitchout, you'll have a good chance to throw one of them out.

If you're wrong, there'll be a 3-2 count, and you'll have to give a good hitter a good pitch to hit. It might be better to try for a strikeout now.

- To call for a pitchout, turn to page 14.
- To call for a strike, turn to page 20.

13

"Ed Neighbor is into his windup, and there go the baserunners. The hit-and-run is on! But wait, the Kid has called for a pitchout! He steps out, grabs the ball, and fires a strike to third baseman Kevin Finley, who nails a sliding Lonnie Snyder."

"Wow! Great call by the Kid, Tim, and just after he came into the game. The Barons have had their problems hitting Ed Neighbor, and manager Buddy Phipps was trying to score two runs on one hit. But the Kid read his mind. Ed Neighbor keeps his shutout going. Blue Sox 2, Barons 0!"

*The game moves along, with neither team scoring, to the bottom of the eighth inning.*

"The Blue Sox are trying to add to a 2-0 lead. And thanks to singles by Denny Hill and Rusty Mills, sandwiched around a groundout by Stroke Thurman, the Sox have runners on the corners with one out and the Kid coming up."

"The Kid is taking a long, hard look at third-base coach Ron Cron, Tim. The Kid wants to see if there's a play on here."

| Batter | Balls | Strikes | Outs |
|--------|-------|---------|------|
| The Kid, C | 0 | 0 | 1 |

Time to think. The Barons are looking for the bunt and will probably put on a rotation play. That means the shortstop will cover third so the third baseman can field the bunt. The second baseman will cover second.

This might be a good time to try a suicide squeeze. Denny would take off from third on the pitch and you would have to bunt the ball. Then again, Denny is slow. Maybe a fake bunt would work better. The fake would get the infielders moving, then you'd take a full swing and try to hit the ball through the infield.

THE KID

Third-base coach Ron Cron looks confused. He can't tell if Grampa is flashing a sign or just rubbing his belly. You signal the baserunners with *your* call.

- To try the suicide squeeze, turn to page 16.
- To try the fake bunt, turn to page 22.

15

"The Barons put on the rotation play. Ken Rhodes winds up . . . and Denny Hill breaks for home! The Kid bunts! It's a suicide squeeze!

"Catcher Buzz Saw Bradshaw fields the bunt in a flash, and Denny Hill slams on the brakes. Bradshaw runs him back toward third and tags him out. Rusty Mills moves over to second and the Kid is safe at first. Well, what do you make of that, Steve?"

"Not the best play there, Tim. The Barons were looking for the bunt, and a suicide squeeze should be a surprise. It also helps to have a jackrabbit on third, and Denny Hill is more like a water buffalo."

"Hector Peña is the batter, Steve. He taps a grounder to shortstop Vince Rizzo. The throw to first is in time, and the Blue Sox are out. At the end of eight, they still lead, 2-0."

*The game goes to the ninth, with the Barons at bat.*

"Ed Neighbor has gotten into some trouble here, Steve. He walked Buzz Saw Bradshaw to lead off the inning. Coming up is Walt Metcalf, who has 24 home runs this season. The Kid calls time and heads for the mound."

Inning: 9     At Bat: Barons
Score: Blue Sox 2, Barons 0

| Batter | Balls | Strikes | Outs |
|--------|-------|---------|------|
| Metcalf, 1B | 0 | 0 | 0 |

Ed Neighbor has pitched a great game, but he's tired. If one of his pitches gets away from him, Metcalf can do some damage. It's time to pull Ed and go for a relief pitcher, a closer.

Here's the question. Should you bring in righty fastballer Alan Sorensen, even though Metcalf is a lefty? Or do you bring in lefty Ned Kelly, who has great control and pitches more like Ed Neighbor? Think about the things you considered when you chose a starting pitcher *(see page 9)*.

THE KID

You can't ask Grampa for help. He and Grumpy Sternemann are reminiscing about the time they put pine tar in Red Schoendienst's cap. It's your call.

- To bring in Alan Sorensen, turn to page 27.
- To bring in Ned Kelly, turn to page 18.

"The Kid tugs on his left ear. Here comes southpaw reliever Ned Kelly to face the Barons with one man on and nobody out. Lefty Walt Metcalf steps into the batter's box. Kelly kicks and deals. The curveball breaks over the inside corner of the plate for strike one."

"Whew! Ned had Metcalf bailing out on that one, Tim."

"The next pitch looks like the same high and inside curve. Metcalf just watches it for strike two. The third pitch is another inside curve . . . a swing and a miss. Strike three!"

"Three pitches, three strikes, one out, Tim. And here's another lefty slugger, Ace Edwards."

"Ned's first pitch to Edwards is a slider low and outside. Edwards grounds a one-hopper to short-stop Speedy Green. Speedy flips to Hector Peña at second, who steps on the bag and throws on to Denny Hill at first. Double play and — just like that — the ball game is over! The Blue Sox win it, 2-0. Chalk up a save for Ned Kelly and a win for Ed Neighbor."

BLUE SOX WIN!

18

"Baron pitcher Ken Rhodes checks the runners. Here's the windup, the pitch . . . strike, right on the outside corner. The count is now full at 3-2."

"Speedy Green was taking all the way on that one, Tim. Too bad. That was a good pitch to hit. With the game on the line, a batter's got to hit the ball!"

"Right you are, Steve Daniels. Ken Rhodes winds up. He throws low and inside. Green 'golfs' it to left. Lonnie Snyder grabs the fly ball for the out, and now the Blue Sox are down to their final out. Denny Hill is the batter, and he swings at the first pitch . . . and hits one deep down the rightfield line! It might be . . . it could be . . . it's . . . a foul ball. Strike one. Denny looks at the second pitch for strike two."

"Uh-oh, Tim. Rhodes has Denny dancing on a hot plate now."

"The Metropolitan Park crowd is roaring. Here's the pitch . . . a swing and a miss for strike three. The ball game is over. It's a heartbreaker for the Blue Sox, as they go down in defeat, 3-2."

## BARONS WIN

"All right, Steve. The Kid is in the game for Cal Scott. He flashes Ed Neighbor the signal. Eddie winds up, and there go the runners. Here's the pitch. It's a fastball over the plate. Edwards swings . . . and hits a high fly ball to rightfield. It's way back there! Rightfielder Stroke Thurman leaps . . . but the ball just clears the fence for a three-run homer! The Barons take the lead, 3-2."

"Tim, with the count 2-2, Edwards was looking for a pitch right over the plate. When a hitter guesses right, his chances of hitting the ball hard go way up. And when a lefthanded batter hits the ball hard in this park — watch out!"

"Herm Davis is up next, Steve. He taps an easy grounder back to Ed Neighbor. Eddie tosses to first to retire the side."

*The score stays Barons 3, Blue Sox 2 through the next inning and a half, and the game moves to the bottom of the eighth. The Blue Sox are batting.*

"The Blue Sox are running out of time, Steve. They need to get something going right now."

"Well, they're off to a good start, Tim. Rusty Mills drew a walk, and now the Kid is up with a 1-1 count."

You're concentrating hard at the plate. Rusty is the tying run, and your job is to advance him to second or third.

The first pitch was a ball, high and outside. The second pitch looked high but was called a strike. There's a good chance the next pitch will be low. That would be a good pitch to bunt. You could sacrifice Rusty to second.

**THE KID**

Or, you could try a hit-and-run play. Rusty would run on the pitch, and you would try to hit the ball on the ground. A groundout would get him to second and a single could get him to third. But a line-out could turn into a double play.

Grampa's at the water cooler. This is your call. You signal Rusty, then dig in.

- To bunt, turn to page 24.
- To hit-and-run, turn to page 23.

"The Barons are in their bunt defense. Here's the pitch by Ken Rhodes. The Kid squares . . . no, the Kid swings away and lines a base hit through the gap where J.R. James usually stands! Denny Hill scores! Rusty Mills races around to third and the Kid is standing at first with a big, big single."

"A 3-0 lead for the Blue Sox, Tim! The Kid saw an opportunity and took it!"

"Hector Peña is up now, Steve. And the first pitch is hit deep to right. Ace Edwards is going back . . . back . . . back . . . back . . . oh, and he makes the catch at the warning track. Rusty Mills watches him from third, then tags up and scores easily to give the Blue Sox a 4-0 lead! Kevin Finley flies to center to end the inning, but the damage has been done."

"The Barons are going to have a tough time coming back from four runs down the way Eddie Neighbor has been pitching today, Tim."

*And the Barons do have a tough time. They go down in order in the top of the ninth.*

BLUE SOX WIN!

"Here's the pitch . . . and there goes Rusty Mills! The Kid hits a low line drive right over first base! It gets past Ace Edwards and rolls into the corner. Rusty scores, and the Kid chugs into second with a double! Tie game, 3-3!"

"Fine piece of hitting, Tim. The Kid hit the ball behind Rusty, which always gives a runner a better chance to advance."

"Hector Peña is up. The Kid is the go-ahead run at second. The first pitch is a change-up inside . . . and Hector cracks it down the third-base line! Lonnie Snyder runs the ball down, but the Kid scores easily. Hector slides into second with a double! The Sox take the lead, 4-3!"

"Holy cow, Tim. Listen to this sellout crowd! "

"Hector takes a short lead off second. Here's the pitch to Kevin Finley . . . and Kevin lines one . . . oh, right at shortstop Vince Rizzo! Rizzo steps on second base to double-up Hector. Neighbor whiffs to retire the side, but the Blue Sox still lead."

*With the fans on their feet, Ed Neighbor mows down the Barons 1-2-3 in the top of the ninth.*

BLUE SOX WIN!

"Here's the pitch. The Kid squares to . . . uh-oh, the Kid bunts it into the air. Rhodes grabs it for the out. Rusty Mills holds at first. One down here in the eighth."

"That was a weird call, Tim. Down by a run with no outs near the end of a game, a team should play to win, not to tie. The Kid should have been trying to hit the ball hard."

"Easy now, Steve. Hector Peña is at the plate . . . and he hits a grounder to short. It could be two! Vince Rizzo flips to J.R. James at second, who fires to Walt Metcalf at first for the double play. That retires the Blue Sox in the bottom of the eighth, down 3-2."

*The Barons go down in order in the top of the ninth and the game moves to the bottom of the ninth.*

"The Blue Sox are down to their last chance, but a single by pinch-hitter Mike Gilmore and a walk to Harold Carlson have put runners on first and second with one out. And now Baron pitcher Ken Rhodes has gone behind in the count, 3-1, to Speedy Green.

"It's hero time for Speedy Green, Tim."

24

| Batter | Balls | Strikes | Outs |
|--------|-------|---------|------|
| Green, SS | 3 | 1 | 1 |

Speedy looks over for the play. Rhodes has been careful, because Speedy is so good with the bat. But now he must throw a strike.

The pitches to Speedy have all been inside. Rhodes probably will throw outside next. The outfield is playing deep but toward left, because Speedy is a righthanded hitter. You could signal Speedy to cross up the defense and hit to the opposite field. Or you could have him take the pitch and hope for a walk. That would bring up Denny Hill with the bases loaded. You ask Grampa what he thinks.

**THE KID**

"Think? I think Warren Gamaliel Harding was a much better president than he ever gets credit for being — that's what I think, Kid!" Grampa came out of leftfield with that one. You're on your own here.

- To have Speedy hit to the opposite field, turn to page 26.
- To have Speedy take the pitch, turn to page 19.

25

TIM

"Okay, folks, here we go! Baron pitcher Ken Rhodes gives Mike Gilmore a look at second and Harold Carlson a look at first. He sets and throws. Speedy swings . . . and it's a line drive into the rightfield corner! Rightfielder Ace Edwards is going to have to chase it down. Gilmore is rounding third, with Carlson close behind. Second baseman J.R. James takes the throw from Edwards and relays the ball home. Gilmore scores! Carlson scores! The game is over! The Blue Sox win, 4-3! "

"Good planning and great hitting there, Tim. There's an old saying, "Hit the ball where it's pitched." Well, a fine hitter like Speedy Green can do just that, and outside pitches are likely to go to the opposite field. That was smart baseball."

"And it looks like the Blue Sox are thanking the Kid for that quick think-ing, Steve. The whole team is congrat-ulating the Kid for this great victory."

STEVE

BLUE SOX WIN!

"Righty hurler Alan Sorensen completes his warmup tosses, Steve, and we're set to go. Lefty slugger Walt Metcalf digs in at the plate. The first two pitches are low and inside."

"Alan's being too careful, Tim. Now that he's behind in the count, 2-0, he needs to throw a strike but not make it so good that Metcalf can clobber it."

"Alan winds, delivers . . . and that ball is hit deep to rightfield! Stroke Thurman goes back . . . back . . . but that ball is history! A two-run home for Walt Metcalf."

"That was a good fastball, Tim, but it was right over the plate. Now, we have a tie ballgame."

"Ace Edwards is the next batter, Steve. Edwards swings . . . and hits a high fly ball way out to centerfield! The fans are on their feet! But centerfielder Rusty Mills can only watch as the ball lands 20 rows back in the bleachers! Back-to-back home runs, and the Barons take the lead, 3-2. My oh my, what a comeback!"

*The Barons' next three hitters go down in order. But so do the Blue Sox in the bottom of the ninth.*

## BARONS WIN

27

"Rhodes throws. Ed Neighbor swings . . . and hits the ball almost straight up in the air. Shortstop Vince Rizzo calls for the ball and makes the catch. Two down."

"Sometimes you have to let your pitcher take his cuts, Tim, but it's awfully hard when he's facing someone like Ken Rhodes."

"Here comes Harold Carlson. Here's the pitch . . . low and *way* outside for ball one. Looked like that one got away from Rhodes, Steve."

"No, Tim, that was a setup pitch. Rhodes wanted to give Harold a reason to look for a pitch outside so he could cross him up with something inside."

"Here's the next pitch. Rhodes zips one inside . . . and Harold pops it up behind the plate. Buzz Saw Bradshaw makes the catch. The side is retired and we're still scoreless after three."

*Neither team scores in the fourth and fifth innings, and the game moves to the top of the sixth.*

"The Barons are threatening here, on a triple by Herm Davis. With one out, Rodney Hammond is up with a 2-0 count and a chance to put — "

"Pardon me, Tim, but it looks like there's a commotion in the Blue Sox dugout!"

| Batter | Balls | Strikes | Outs |
|--------|-------|---------|------|
| Hammond, 3B | 2 | 0 | 1 |

*Ring!* There's the dugout phone. Grampa answers it.

"Graff speaking. She what? He'll be right there." Grampa climbs the dugout steps and calls for time. "Cal, get over here!"

Catcher Cal Scott trots over to Grampa. Then Cal heads for the showers.

"Cal's wife had triplets!" Grampa says. "Put your gear on, Kid. You're going in."

You think fast as you trot onto the field. There's one out, Herm Davis is on third, and Rodney Hammond is at bat with a 2-0 count.

THE KID

Hammond's batting average is low, but he does have power. Maybe you should walk him intentionally. That would bring up the pitcher with runners on first and third and a chance for a double play. Or you could take your chances with Hammond.

- To walk Hammond, turn to page 30.
- To pitch to Hammond, turn to page 52.

"The Kid replaces Cal Scott at catcher, Steve. And it looks like the Blue Sox are going to give Rodney Hammond a free pass and pitch to Ken Rhodes with runners on the corners and one out."

"That's a good call, Tim. In a close game, you want to keep that runner on third from scoring. And this creates a double-play possibility with the weakest hitter in the Baron lineup coming up."

"Ed Neighbor winds, throws . . . and Rhodes grounds one to shortstop Speedy Green. Speedy tosses to Hector Peña at second, who fires to first. Double play! The Blue Sox escape that jam, and after five and a half innings, we have no score."

*The game remains scoreless going into the bottom of the seventh inning. The Blue Sox are batting.*

"The Blue Sox have something going here, sports fans. Rusty Mills is on third with a one-out triple and the Kid is at the plate, facing Ken Rhodes with a 1-2 count."

"The Kid's done a great job behind the plate since coming in for Cal Scott, Tim. Let's see if the Kid can help the team with his bat, too."

| Batter | Balls | Strikes | Outs |
|--------|-------|---------|------|
| The Kid, C | 1 | 2 | 1 |

Okay, the game's scoreless in the seventh. What can you do to help get this run across?

Ken Rhodes is a classic "setup" pitcher. That means he'll throw the first few pitches to one area of the strike zone to set you up and get you expecting another one in the same place. Then he'll throw to a different area and catch you by surprise. His first two pitches were inside, so he'll probably go outside with the next one.

You can hear the fans cheering, and you'd love to hit a home run. You could try to pull the next pitch over the leftfield fence. Or maybe you should just go for the single, and hit the ball hard where it's pitched.

- To swing for the fences, turn to page 42.
- To go with the pitch, turn to page 32.

31

"Rhodes winds up. Here's the pitch to the Kid . . . and the Kid lines a base hit into rightfield! Rusty Mills crosses the plate and the Blue Sox break the scoreless tie."

"The Kid went with that outside pitch, Tim. The Kid did just what was needed to drive in the go-ahead run."

"Hector Peña steps up to the plate now, Steve. And he lines the first pitch to leftfield, but it's caught by Lonnie Snyder. The Kid stays at first. Two outs, and Kevin Finley is the batter. He hits a one-hopper to third baseman Rodney Hammond. Hammond gets the force at second that ends the inning, but not before the Blue Sox go ahead, 1-0."

*The Barons come up in the eighth inning.*

"It's looking like the Blue Sox may need more than one run to win this game, Steve. Back-to-back hits by Ace Edwards and Herm Davis have given the Barons runners on first and third with one out."

"The bottom third of the Baron order is coming up, Tim, and those are the team's weakest hitters. Manager Buddy Phipps might try a trick play here to get a run across."

| Batter | Balls | Strikes | Outs |
|--------|-------|---------|------|
| Rizzo, SS | 0 | 0 | 1 |

THE KID

You check out the field. With runners on first and third and less than two outs, the Barons are in a perfect setup for a double steal. Davis would take off for second on the pitch, and then Edwards would break for home, putting you in a real fix.

A smart ballplayer anticipates what he will do in a situation before it happens. If the Barons try a double steal, should you hold on to the ball and try to tag Edwards out? Or, would it be better to throw to second baseman Hector Peña to get Davis, and hope Hector can get the ball back to you quickly if Edwards tries for home? You'd better decide now because Ed Neighbor is ready to pitch to the batter, Vince Rizzo.

- To go after the runner on third, turn to page 34.
- To throw down to second, turn to page 38.

"Here's the pitch. Davis is running! It's a double steal! The Kid fakes a throw to second . . . and here comes Edwards trying to score from third! The Kid charges up the third-base line and tags Edwards out!"

"The Kid played that like a 10-year veteran, Tim! He drew Edwards in with the fake and then ran him back to third before making the tag! Davis is on second, but there are two outs."

"Okay, Tim, and the second pitch to Vince Rizzo is lined into leftfield for a single. Harold Carlson fields it quickly and holds Davis at third. The next batter, Rodney Hammond, pops the ball up near third base. Kevin Finley catches it to retire the side."

*The Blue Sox don't score in the eighth inning, and the game moves to the ninth. The Sox lead 1-0.*

"With one out, Ed Neighbor has given up a single to Lonnie Snyder and walked J.R. James. And the heart of the Baron order is coming up, beginning with Buzz Saw Bradshaw."

"Reliever Alan Sorensen is loosening up in the bullpen, Tim. And the Kid is headed for the mound. But first Bradshaw has something to say."

34

| Batter | Balls | Strikes | Outs |
|--------|-------|---------|------|
| Bradshaw, C | 0 | 0 | 1 |

"Pack up your toys and go home, Kid. I'm taking the next pitch downtown."

Buzz Saw Bradshaw is a windbag, but he's also a good hitter. Bradshaw hasn't reached base, but he did hit Ed's pitches hard twice today. He has good power *and* the third highest batting average on the Barons. He can hit a variety of pitches well.

Ed Neighbor is good at getting power hitters to swing at his pitches and fly out. The batter after Bradshaw is big Walt Metcalf, whom Ed has handled all day long. Ed might be tiring, but his momentum could carry him through.

**THE KID**

On the other hand, you could bring in fastballer Alan Sorensen. Alan could probably over-power Bradshaw *and* Metcalf.

- To bring in closer Alan Sorensen, turn to 36.
- To let Ed Neighbor finish the game, turn to 41.

35

"The Blue Sox aren't taking any chances here, Tim. Alan Sorensen is coming into the game to face Buzz Saw Bradshaw."

"Alan takes his warm-ups, Steve, and he's ready to go. Bradshaw steps in. Alan winds up with his famous high leg kick. Here's the pitch . . . strike one. Wow! That is some kind of heat. Here's the second pitch . . . a swing and a miss for strike two. And the third pitch . . . swing and a miss, strike three!

"We're one out away from a Blue Sox win, Tim, and here's Walt Metcalf."

"Alan burns one past him for a strike. Here's the second pitch. Metcalf swings and misses — strike two. This sellout crowd is on its feet. Metcalf digs in, Alan kicks and fires . . . strike three! The ball game is over. The Blue Sox win, 1-0."

"Holy cow, Tim! A combined shutout by Eddie Neighbor and Alan Sorensen against the best long-ball-hitting team in the league. And credit's got to go to the Kid, too. The Kid caught a smart game coming off the bench."

BLUE SOX WIN!

"Here's the delivery, and there goes Rusty Mills, running with the pitch. The Kid swings and . . . oh, no, the Kid lined it right at second baseman J.R. James! James throws to shortstop Vince Rizzo, and Rusty Mills is doubled-off second base. That's the game, Steve Daniels. The Barons win, 2-1."

"Tough break for the Kid and for the Blue Sox, Tim. The Kid got a good pitch to hit but not a good pitch to hit on the ground. It was hit hard, but right at J.R. James, who turned it into an easy double play. The hit-and-run was a gutsy call. It just didn't work today.

"Why, look over there, Tim. Buddy Phipps is coming out of the Baron dugout to pat the Kid on the back. Buddy is one manager who loves a fighter, and the Kid showed plenty of fight today. The Kid will be back, Tim, just you watch."

## BARONS WIN

37

"Ed Neighbor winds up, and here's the pitch. Davis takes off for second! The double steal is on. The Kid throws to second . . . and here comes Edwards trying to score from third! Davis is safe at second. Hector Peña throws back to the Kid and . . . Edwards is safe at home! We have a tie ball game."

"Tim, that's a tough play for a catcher. But you have to keep that runner on third from scoring, even if it means letting the other runner steal second."

"That pitch was called a ball, Steve, so the count is 1-0 on Vince Rizzo. Rizzo swings at the next pitch . . . and lines it into rightfield for a base hit! Here comes Davis around third. He'll score easily. The Barons lead 2-1. Rodney Hammond flies to leftfield and Ken Rhodes strikes out to end the inning."

*Both teams fail to score in their next at-bats. The game moves to the bottom of the ninth.*

"The Blue Sox are trailing 2-1 here in the ninth. But thanks to a one-out double by Rusty Mills, they have a runner in scoring position. The Kid is at bat with a 3-1 count."

| Batter | Balls | Strikes | Outs |
|--------|-------|---------|------|
| The Kid, C | 3 | 1 | 1 |

The game is on the line. Rusty is the tying run on second. You have to get a hit.

The count is 3-1, so Ken Rhodes can only throw strikes. How about a hit-and-run play? Rusty will take off the instant the ball leaves the pitcher's hand. You must hit the ball — preferably on the ground. If it works, Rusty would reach third and maybe even score. But it could also lead to a double play.

**THE KID**

Then again, maybe you should just try for a solid hit. The outfield is playing deep and toward left, the first and third basemen are guarding the foul lines, hoping to prevent a double down the line. A hit could also get Rusty home, and it would put you on base, too.

- To play hit-and-run, turn to page 37.
- To go for the hit, turn to page 40.

"Rusty Mills takes a short lead off second. Rhodes goes into his windup, here's the pitch … and it's hit deep to right centerfield! Ace Edwards isn't going to get to this one. It's rolling all the way to the wall! Rusty Mills is rounding third and the Kid is rounding first. Edwards picks up the ball and throws it in to second baseman J.R. James. Rusty Mills scores, and the Kid is safe at second!"

"The Kid got a good pitch to hit, Tim, and clobbered it. That was the kind of situation a batter loves to be in. We have a 2-2 ballgame, and now the Kid is the winning run at second."

"Hector Peña is the batter for the Blue Sox, Steve. Ken Rhodes sets, and delivers. It's a ground ball, up the middle. It gets past Rhodes and rolls just beyond the reach of shortstop Vince Rizzo into centerfield. The Kid is around third and hightailing it home. Herm Davis scoops up the ball and rifles it to the plate. The Kid slides . . . safe! The Blue Sox win it, 3-2!"

BLUE SOX WIN!

"Ed Neighbor has pitched a tough one today, Steve Daniels, and he is going to stay in the game. Buzz Saw Bradshaw steps into the batter's box. Ed takes the sign from the Kid, checks the runners, and throws. Bradshaw swings . . . and launches a fly ball, deep to right centerfield . . . open the window, Aunt Minnie, because that ball is . . . out of here! A three-run homer for Wayne Bradshaw, and the Barons take a 3-1 lead."

"I think Ed meant to throw an outside curveball, Tim, but the pitch floated out over the plate where Bradshaw could take a nice poke at it. That's what happens when a pitcher gets tired."

"Okay, Steve, and here's Walt Metcalf. He swings at the first pitch and hits a towering fly to leftfield, where it is caught by Harold Carlson for the second out. Ace Edwards steps up to the plate, and he lofts an easy fly ball to rightfield. Stroke Thurman grabs it, and we go to the bottom of the ninth with the Barons now leading by two runs."

*The Blue Sox can't bounce back this time. They go down in order in the bottom of the ninth.*

## BARONS WIN

"Ken Rhodes sets, and throws. The Kid takes a big cut . . . and hits a ground ball to third. Rodney Hammond gloves it, holds Rusty Mills at third, and fires on to first. Two down."

"Tim, the Kid was trying so hard to win the game all by himself that he tried to pull a ball over the outside part of the plate. Trying to pull an outside pitch usually results in an easy ground ball to the infield. It's better to try and hit an outside pitch to the oppo-site field."

"Hector Peña at bat, Steve. Rhodes throws . . . and Hector pops it up. Second baseman J.R. James floats over into short rightfield and grabs it for the third out. We're still scoreless at the end of seven.

*The game moves to the top of the eighth.*

"Eddie Neighbor is showing signs of tiring here, Steve. With one out, Lonnie Snyder ripped a single to left and then stole second. J.R. James is at the plate with a 1-1 count."

"Good speed on second and a good hitter at the plate, Tim. Let's see if the Sox can stop the Barons here."

Inning: 8    At Bat: Barons
Score: Barons 0, Blue Sox 0

| Batter | Balls | Strikes | Outs |
|---|---|---|---|
| James, 2B | 1 | 1 | 1 |

You'd better plan ahead so you'll be ready for anything.

If James hits a single, Snyder will try to score. Your outfielders will throw the ball home, but your infielders will be ready to cut off the throw — that is, to catch the throw before it goes through. You would have to decide if the outfielder's throw has a chance to nab Snyder at the plate, or if it would better for the infielder to cut off the throw and hold James at first.

Here's the pitch, and James singles to center. Snyder is rounding third and James is almost at first. Centerfielder Rusty Mills fields the ball and comes up throwing. Should you yell to second baseman Hector Peña to to let the throw go through or to cut it off?

THE KID

- To have Hector let the throw come home, turn to page 48.
- To have Hector cut off the throw, turn to page 44.

43

"Hector Peña cuts off Rusty Mills's throw from centerfield. Snyder scores, and James is held at first. A smart play, Steve. It didn't look like Hector's throw would have been in time."

"It's tempting to try to save the shutout, Tim. But if the throw had gone home, the Blue Sox would still be down by a run, and James would be in scoring position."

"Buzz Saw Bradshaw steps up to bat, Steve. Ed Neighbor pitches, and Bradshaw hits a fly ball, deep to center. Rusty Mills goes back to the warning track … and makes the catch! James holds at first. Two outs, and Walt Metcalf swaggers up to the plate. Ed Neighbor throws . . . and Metcalf hits another fly ball to center. Rusty is under it, and he has it for the third out. The Barons lead the Blue Sox, 1-0."

*Neither team scores in its next at-bat, and the game moves to the bottom of the ninth inning.*

"Well, Steve, the Kid has gotten something going for the Blue Sox with a one-out single to left field. Hector Peña is the next batter."

"The Blue Sox will need some smart base-running by the Kid to tie up this game, Tim."

| Batter | Balls | Strikes | Outs |
|--------|-------|---------|------|
| Peña, 2B | 0 | 0 | 1 |

You're the tying run. Time to plan ahead again.

If Hector hits the ball to the infield, you'll burn over to second and try to break up the double play. If he singles to leftfield, you'll probably have to hold at second. But if he singles to center or right, you might be able to go to third. You'll have to watch third-base coach Ron Cron. It's his job to watch the field so you can concentrate on running.

**THE KID**

Here comes the pitch . . . and Hector raps a single to rightfield. Start running! Okay, you're going to make second easily. Ron Cron is signaling for you to hold up, but the crowd is urging you on. You want to go to third. What should you do?

- To stop at second, turn to page 46.
- To try for third, turn to page 51.

45

"Baron second baseman J.R. James catches Ace Edwards's throw from right and spins, but the Kid stops at second. Hector is on at first!"

"That was good baserunning, Tim! As much as the Kid wanted to go to third, the Kid knows you have to listen to the coach. The coach has a better view of the field. Now we have a rally going."

"Kevin Finley is the batter, Steve. Here's the pitch . . . and Finley hits a soft line drive to right center. It's going to drop in for a hit! Ron Cron is waving the Kid home. Ace Edwards grabs the ball. Here's his throw . . . too late! The Kid scores the tying run! Hector moves over to third, and Kevin is safe on first!

"Mike Gilmore is pinch-hitting for Ed Neighbor, Tim."

"Here's the pitch . . . and Mike hits a fly ball, deep to centerfield! Hector has gone back to tag the third-base bag so he can run if the ball is caught. Herm Davis makes the catch. Here comes Hector. Here's the throw. Not in time! Hector scores! The Blue Sox win, 2-1!"

BLUE SOX WIN!

46

"Catcher Buzz Saw Bradshaw signals pitcher Ken Rhodes. Rhodes shakes off the sign, shakes off another, now he nods. Rhodes sets. Here's the windup . . . and a pitch high and inside. The Kid bunts it! The ball takes a high bounce to the left, where Rhodes fields it. He throws to J.R. James at second, and James fires to Walt Metcalf at first for an easy double play! And just like that, Steve, the Blue Sox go from threatening for a win to being just one out away from a loss."

"A batter shouldn't be too cautious in the bottom of the ninth, down by two runs, Tim. A high inside pitch is awfully hard to bunt well, too."

"Hector Peña steps up, with two away and a runner on third. Rhodes throws . . . and Hector flies to leftfield. Leftfielder Lonnie Synder makes the catch for the third out. A tough ninth inning, Steve, and the Blue Sox drop this one to the Barons, 2-0."

## BARONS WIN

47

"Here comes Lonnie Snyder trying to score! Here's the throw home . . . too late . . . Snyder crosses the plate standing up. James takes second, and the Barons lead, 1-0."

"The Sox didn't have a chance to get Snyder, Tim. If Hector had cut off the throw, James would be on first instead of second."

"Next up is Buzz Saw Bradshaw, Steve. Here's the pitch . . . and Bradshaw grounds one up the middle . . . oh, what a grab by shortstop Speedy Green! He fires on to first to nip Bradshaw. James crosses over to third, and that brings up Ace Edwards with two outs. There's a single up the middle! James will score. Uh-oh, Edwards is trying to stretch it into a double! Here's the throw from centerfielder Rusty Mills . . . Edwards slides . . . he's out! The side is retired, but the Barons now lead, 2-0.

*Neither team scores in its next at-bat, and the game moves to the bottom of the ninth.*

"The Blue Sox are trying to climb back into this one. A single by Stroke Thurman and a walk to Rusty Mills have given them runners on first and second with no outs. The Kid is up, with a 2-2 count. The Kid represents the winning run."

| At Bat | Balls | Strikes | Outs |
|--------|-------|---------|------|
| The Kid, C | 2 | 2 | 0 |

You've got to be aggressive here. Now think hard what to do.

The pitcher has thrown you four outside pitches, so there's a good chance he'll come inside with the next one. You can hit outside pitches to the opposite field, but your real strength is any pitch inside. This is an almost ideal time to swing for the fences.

**THE KID**

Wait a second, the infield is playing back. Maybe you should play it safe and bunt for a hit. It would load the bases with no outs. You check the dugout to see what Grampa Graff thinks. Oh, he's taping you with his video camera. What do you do?

- To bunt for a hit, turn to page 47.
- To swing away, turn to page 50.

"This Metropolitan Park crowd has come alive, Tim! I can't even hear public address announcer Chick Lathers!

"Here we go, Steve. Stroke Thurman has a short lead off second, Rusty Mills takes a step off first. The infield is playing back. Baron pitcher Ken Rhodes shakes off a signal from catcher Buzz Saw Bradshaw, shakes off another, now nods. He winds up, he throws and . . . the Kid hits a rocket to left! It's sailing for the fence! That ball is going . . . going . . . gone! Unbelievable! The Kid hits a three-run homer in the bottom of the ninth to win it for the Blue Sox!

"The Kid really ripped the horsehide off that one, Tim! Rhodes put one right in his wheelhouse and the Kid was ready for it."

"Stroke Thurman, Rusty Mills, and the rest of the Blue Sox are waiting for the Kid at home plate! The Kid rounds third and sprints home. The crowd is going nuts! The Blue Sox win it, 3-2. We've got to make way for the local news. So until next time, I'm Tim Brown for Steve Daniels. So long, everybody!

BLUE SOX WIN!

50

"The Kid rounds second and is trying for third! Baron second baseman J.R. James takes the throw from rightfield, turns, and fires to teammate Rodney Hammond at third. Here's the slide . . . and the Kid is out!"

"The Kid was too eager, Tim, stretching for a base that was out of reach. But the Kid's biggest mistake was running through third-base coach Ron Cron's stop sign. Baserunners have to follow their coaches' directions. Now the Blue Sox have two outs and one baserunner — Hector Peña at first."

STEVE

"And they're down to their last out, too, Steve. Kevin Finley is the batter. Here's the pitch . . . and it's a fly ball to short rightfield. Ace Edwards lines it up. This should be the ball game. Edwards catches it for the final out, and the Blue Sox lose a heartbreaker, 1-0."

TIM

BARONS WIN

"We're going to see the Kid today after all, Steve. The Kid comes in for Cal Scott, gets settled behind the plate, and gives Ed Neighbor the sign. Here's the pitch . . . and Rodney Hammond hits a fly ball to centerfield that's carrying back . . . back . . . back to the fence, where Rusty Mills grabs it for the out. Herm Davis, who was watching from third base, tags up and jogs home. The Barons take a 1-0 lead."

"Behind in the count, Eddie Neighbor threw that pitch right down Broadway, Tim, and Hammond got most of it. This old ballpark was just big enough to hold that shot."

"Ken Rhodes fans to retire the side, Steve. But the score in the middle of the sixth inning is Barons 1, Blue Sox 0."

*The score remains the same, as the game moves to the bottom of the eighth.*

"Back-to-back singles by Harold Carlson and Speedy Green have given the Blue Sox a scoring threat with one out here in the eighth."

"Denny Hill, one of the Blue Sox' smartest hitters, is at the plate, Tim. He's behind in the count, 1-2, and waiting for a sign."

| Batter | Balls | Strikes | Outs |
|--------|-------|---------|------|
| Hill, 1B | 1 | 2 | 1 |

Okay, you've got fast runners on base and a good batter in a tough hitting situation. What does that say to you? How about a trick play, like a delayed double steal? When pitcher Ken Rhodes sets on the mound, Speedy would run for second. Just after Speedy takes off, Harold would race for home. Since Rhodes is a lefty, he sets facing first base, so he wouldn't see Harold take off and would probably throw to second. Speedy would be out, but Harold would score, tying the game.

**THE KID**

Then again, Rhodes might not fall for such a trick. Maybe it would be better to forget the steal and just let Denny do what he does best — swing the bat.

– To have Denny swing away, turn to page 54.
– To try a delayed double steal, turn to page 61.

53

"Ken Rhodes sets on the mound, and here's the pitch . . . Denny Hill lines a single to leftfield! Harold Carlson will score! Lonnie Snyder fields the ball and throws to third baseman Rodney Hammond. Speedy Green is standing up on third and Denny Hill is safe at first."

"Nice piece of hitting by Denny Hill, Tim. That's just good old country hardball. He got a good pitch and smacked it."

"Stroke Thurman is the batter now, Steve. And he hits a high fly ball to deep centerfield. Herm Davis has it lined up. Speedy Green will tag up; he's standing on third base, ready to run as soon as Davis makes the catch. Here comes Speedy, and he scores easily! The Blue Sox take the lead, 2-1. The next batter, Rusty Mills, lines Rhodes's first pitch right into the glove of shortstop Vince Rizzo to retire the side. But the Blue Sox take the lead, 2-1.

*The game moves to the top of the ninth inning.*

"Lonnie Snyder, the Barons' top hitter, leads off, as his team tries to stay in this game."

"The Kid calls for time, Tim. Looks like we may have a pitching change."

54

| Batter | Balls | Strikes | Outs |
|--------|-------|---------|------|
| Snyder, LF | 0 | 0 | 0 |

Ed Neighbor has had a great game, but his warm-up pitches don't have any snap. You decide he's done. Whom do you replace him with? Grampa Graff's cleaning his glasses over there on the bench. Go ask him.

"Well, Kid, take a look at who the Barons have coming up next. Three righties, right? That means you can't go to lefthander Ned Kelly. So that leaves righthanders Ron Richter and Alan Sorensen. Alan's got the heat and Ron's got an arsenal of different pitches. Now check out the high batting averages of the next three Baron hitters. Would it be better to overpower them or try to keep them off-balance with breaking pitches? That's what you have to decide, Kid."

- To bring in Alan Sorensen, turn to page 58.
- To bring in Ron Richter, turn to page 56.

"Ron Richter is in to pitch for the Blue Sox. His first batter is Lonnie Snyder. Ron goes into his slow windup and throws . . . strike one, on a curve low and away. Here's the second pitch . . . and Snyder lines a single into leftfield. The next batter, J.R. James, lines a double down the leftfield line! Lonnie Snyder stops at third."

"Ron's pitches aren't fooling anyone, Tim. Now the tying and go-ahead runs are in scoring position."

"And Buzz Saw Bradshaw is the batter, Steve. Bradshaw swings at the first pitch . . . and lines out to the pitcher! The next batter, Walt Metcalf, also swings at the first pitch . . . and grounds a hard single into centerfield! Snyder and James score, and the Barons are out in front again, 3-2. Ace Edwards hits a sharp grounder to shortstop, but Speedy Green scoops it up, steps on second to get Metcalf, and fires to first for a double play. The side is out, but the Blue Sox now trail by a run."

*The game moves to the bottom of the ninth.*

"The Sox are down to their last at-bat, Steve. The Kid is leading off, and the count is 2-2. Let's see if the Kid can get something going."

56

| Batter | Balls | Strikes | Outs |
|--------|-------|---------|------|
| The Kid, C | 2 | 2 | 0 |

It's rally time! Ken Rhodes has two strikes and two balls on you — on two low inside pitches, followed by two high inside pitches. Rhodes likes to set up his pitches, so he'll probably pitch outside here. But the fielders are all playing you to pull. That usually means Rhodes will throw a change-up or an inside pitch.

You can cross up the Barons by hitting the pitch to the opposite field. If you close up your stance, your bat will be at the correct angle to hit an offspeed or inside pitch to rightfield.

Then again, the fielders could just be out of position. To be safe, maybe you should use your regular stance, hit the ball hard, and hope it finds a hole.

**THE KID**

- To hit to right, turn to page 59.
- To just hit the ball hard, turn to page 80.

"Okay, sports fans, Alan Sorensen is in to protect a 2-1 lead and save this game for Ed Neighbor. The right-handed hurler will be facing the top of the Baron order. Lonnie Snyder, J.R. James, and Buzz Saw Bradshaw are as tough a 1-2-3 as any in the majors."

"They sure are, Steve. Here's Alan's windup, and the pitch to Snyder . . . strike one! Wow! That had to be over 100 miles per hour! Here's the second pitch . . . Snyder swings and grounds one back to the mound. Sorensen snags it and tosses to first for the out. The next batter, J.R. James, swings at the first pitch . . . and pops it up behind the plate. The Kid flips off the mask, settles under the ball, and makes the catch. Two away!"

"Old Alan's throwing comets out there, Tim. He was the right reliever for this job."

"Buzz Saw Bradshaw lumbers up to bat, the Baron's last hope. Three fastballs, three swings, three misses, and this ball game is over!"

BLUE SOX WIN!

58

"There's a 2-2 count on the Kid. Ken Rhodes winds up. The pitch is a change-up inside . . . and the Kid punches it down the rightfield line, right between first baseman Walt Metcalf and the bag. Ace Edwards scoops up the ball in the rightfield corner and throws to second baseman J.R. James, but the Kid is safe with an opposite-field double.

"Nice work by the Kid to take that inside pitch the other way, Tim. This late in the game, Metcalf should have been guarding the foul line."

"Hector Peña steps in to hit, Steve. Rhodes pitches . . . and Hector lines a base hit down the leftfield line! The Kid scores and Hector is safe at second with another double! Tie game, and Kevin Finley is the batter. Finley swings . . . and lines a single to left centerfield! Centerfielder Herm Davis is going to have to chase this one down. Here comes Hector trying to score. Here comes the throw from Davis. Hector slides . . . he's safe, and the game is over! The Sox win, 4-3. Talk about your fantastic finishes!

BLUE SOX WIN!

59

"Here's the pitch . . . Hector bunts it, and the Kid takes off from third! Rhodes fields the ball and flips it to catcher Buzz Saw Bradshaw. The Kid tries to scramble back to third, but Bradshaw tags him out. Hector is safe on first. What went wrong there, Steve?"

"Well, Tim, that was a safety squeeze — a tough call in that situation. A squeeze works best when the runner gets a big jump off third and the defense doesn't get a chance to make a play. By going with the safety squeeze, the Sox gave up the big jump and gave the Barons a chance to make a play. For a safety squeeze to work, you need your best bunter at bat and your fastest runner on third."

"Well, Steve, now it's up to Kevin Finley. Rhodes pitches . . . and Kevin hits a fly ball to centerfield. Herm Davis makes the catch. Two outs, and Mike Gilmore will hit for Alan Sorensen. Mike crushes one, deep to right center! Rightfielder Ace Edwards goes back to the fence . . . and he makes the catch."

"Oooh, Mike came so close to saving the day for the Blue Sox, Tim. But the Barons hang on, 5-4."

## BARONS WIN

"Ken Rhodes sets . . . oh, there goes Speedy Green — he's taking off for second! And now Harold Carlson is breaking for the plate! Rhodes spins, looks at Harold, and freezes him in his tracks. Harold scrambles back to third. Now, Rhodes calmly throws to second base. Speedy slides, but he's out by a mile. What was that supposed to be, Steve?"

"That was the old delayed double steal, Tim. You sometimes see it when a lefty's pitching, but a veteran like Ken Rhodes wasn't about to fall for a trick play like that."

STEVE

TIM

"Denny Hill is still at the plate for the Blue Sox, Steve, but now there are two outs and the tying run on third. Rhodes fires. Denny takes a big swing . . . but he pops it up. Shortstop Vince Rizzo waves everyone off . . . and makes the catch. The Blue Sox can't take advantage of a great scoring opportunity. The Barons still lead 1-0, as we go to the ninth.

*That failed trick play will haunt the Blue Sox. Neither team can score in the ninth inning, and the Sox lose a real nail-biter, 1-0.*

## BARONS WIN

61

"Well, Steve Daniels, Hub King was a little rocky as the Blue Sox starter over the first two innings. He was a little wild. His lack of control really hurt him in the second, when he walked Vince Rizzo and gave up a two-run homer to Rodney Hammond."

"The big youngster looks more under control here in the third, Tim. He has retired J.R. James and Buzz Saw Bradshaw, and now has a 1-2 count on Walt Metcalf."

"Here's the pitch to Metcalf, Steve . . . a swing and a miss for strike three, and the side is retired."

"That's more like it. That pitch might have been low, but when a pitcher is ahead in the count, he has the batter at his mercy."

*The game moves to the bottom of the third with the Barons leading the Blue Sox, 2-0.*

"A single by Harold Carlson followed by a walk to Speedy Green has given the Blue Sox runners on first and second with one out. Denny Hill is at the plate with a 1-1 count."

"Denny started to bunt at that last pitch, Tim, but he took it for a ball. Let's see what the Blue Sox have up their sleeves."

62

| Batter | Balls | Strikes | Outs |
|--------|-------|---------|------|
| Hill, 1B | 1 | 1 | 1 |

"Hey, Kid, coach third base the rest of this inning," Grampa Graff says. "We're going to try a fake bunt . It could shake things up the way those clams shook up my stomach."

Grampa's right. The Barons are putting the rotation play on. J.R. James will cover second and Vince Rizzo will cover third, to free up Rodney Hammond to field the bunt. The outfield is playing shallow. Denny will act as if he's going to bunt again, then take a good swing at the pitch.

**THE KID**

If Denny gets a hit, you'll need to know if you're going to send one runner or both runners home. The infielders will be out of position, so it might be hard for them to make a good relay throw. Then again, maybe you should play it safe.

- To hold Speedy at third, turn to page 82.
- To wave both Harold and Speedy home, turn to page 64.

"There goes the Kid in to coach third base, Steve. Denny Hill squares to bunt . . . no, he swings at the pitch and hits it deep to rightfield! It's going over Ace Edwards's head and rolling all the way to the wall! Harold Carlson is rounding third and Speedy Green is rounding second! Edwards picks up the ball and turns to throw, but there's no relay man! Harold scores, and the Kid is waving Speedy home, too. Two runs score, and Denny Hill is at third with a triple."

"Denny drew the Barons into their bunt defense with the fake stance, Tim. When Edwards got the ball, he had nobody to throw to."

"We're tied at 2, Steve, and Stroke Thurman is the batter. He hits a fly ball to right. Denny tags up. Edwards catches this one, but Denny scores easily. Rusty Mills flies out to center to end the inning, but the Sox go ahead, 3-2 !"

*Neither team scores in the fourth or fifth innings.*

"In the top of the sixth, Ace Edwards has led off for the Barons with a double. And there goes catcher Cal Scott to the mound. Oops, Cal tripped on a candy wrapper on the field. He's holding his ankle."

| Batter | Balls | Strikes | Outs |
|--------|-------|---------|------|
| Davis, CF | 0 | 0 | 0 |

"Cal sprained his ankle, Kid, you're going in for him," Grampa says.

Okay, before Cal got hurt, he was going to the mound to see if Hub should stay in the game. Hub had those wild first two innings, and here in the sixth he threw three balls to the leadoff batter and then a fastball straight over the plate that was rapped for a double. We're near the bottom of the Barons' order and Hub should be able to handle them. But reliever Ron Richter is ready in the bullpen and he's a righty — just like the next three batters.

THE KID

"Hurry up and put your equipment on, Kid," Grampa says. "And what do you think? Hub or Ron?"

- To bring in reliever Ron Richter, turn to page 66.
- To leave Hub in the game, go to page 72.

"Well, Steve Daniels, it looks like we'll get to see The Kid after all. The Kid replaces Cal Scott, and Ron Richter is coming in from the bullpen to relieve Hub King."

"Ron's a control pitcher, Tim. He has a good curveball and tricky offspeed pitches."

"Herm Davis steps up to bat for the Barons, with Ace Edwards on second and no outs. Richter winds and throws. It's a curveball away. Davis lunges for it . . . and hits a fly ball to right. Rightfielder Stroke Thurman grabs it for the out. One away. Vince Rizzo swings at Ron's first pitch and bounces an easy grounder to shortstop. Speedy Green gloves it and throws to first. Two away. And here's Rodney Hammond, who homered on a Hub King fastball in the second. Ooh, Hammond strikes out, looking at three curveballs. The score after five and a half innings remains Blue Sox 3, Barons 2."

*The score stays the same through seven innings.*

"We're in the top of the eighth, and the Barons have Herm Davis on second base with a double. There is one out and a 3-2 count on the batter, Vince Rizzo. Let's see how the Blue Sox decide to pitch to Rizzo, Steve."

| | | | |
|---|---|---|---|
| Inning: 8 | | At Bat: Barons | |
| Score: Blue Sox 3, Barons 2 | | | |

| Batter | Balls | Strikes | Outs |
|---|---|---|---|
| Rizzo, SS | 3 | 2 | 1 |

You want to get Vince Rizzo out, but you have to be careful about how you do it. Herm Davis is a fast runner. If Rizzo hits a fly ball deep enough to the outfield, Herm Davis will tag up and advance to third after the catch. It would be better if you could get Rizzo to strike out. That would keep Davis from going to third.

So far you've pitched Rizzo like this: curveball for a swinging strike, fastball for a ball, curveball for a ball, fastball for a strike, curveball for a ball. What pitch might surprise Rizzo here?

- To call for a change–up, turn to page 70.
- To call for a fastball, turn to page 68.

67

"Here's the pitch. It's a fastball . . . and Vince Rizzo lines it into right centerfield for a base hit. Stroke Thurman runs it down, but Herm Davis scores and Rizzo has a double. We have a tie game, folks, and only one out here in the top of the eighth."

"You know, Tim, one of the keys to pitching is knowing how a hitter thinks. Rizzo was looking for a fastball there, and he got one. I think Ron could have fooled him with a change-up or a curveball."

"Rodney Hammond coming up now, Steve. Here's the pitch . . . and it's knocked into leftfield for a base hit. Harold Carlson hustles over to hold Hammond at first, but Rizzo scores. Ken Rhodes grounds into a double play to end the inning, but the Barons take a 4-3 lead."

*Neither team scores in its next at-bat, and the game moves to the bottom of the ninth.*

"Last chance for the Blue Sox, who are down by a run. Rusty Mills is on first with a leadoff walk. And the Kid is at the plate, ahead in the count, 2-0. Let's see what the Kid can do here."

| Batter | Balls | Strikes | Outs |
|--------|-------|---------|------|
| The Kid, C | 2 | 0 | 0 |

You step out of the box to think.
Ken Rhodes tempted you on the first
two pitches with high balls. Now he will
have to throw a strike, and he will probably throw it
low to try to make you ground into a double play. It's a
good time to try to bunt for a hit.

There are some other things you should
notice. First, Ken Rhodes is a lefthanded
pitcher. That means his pitching motion
causes him to fall off the mound to the
third-base side. Second, first baseman
Walt Metcalf is holding Rusty Mills on
first base. The rest of the infielders are
in their usual positions. Okay, Rhodes is
going to throw. It's time to lay down the bunt. The
only question is: Where?

THE KID

- To bunt down the first-base line, turn to page 71.
- To bunt down the third-base line, turn to page 78.

69

"Here's Ron Richter's 3-2 pitch to Vince Rizzo. It's a change-up. Rizzo swings . . . and misses for strike three!"

"Great call by the Kid and a nice pitch by Richter, Tim. Rizzo was looking for the fastball, and the change-up threw his timing off. He was way out in front of that pitch."

"Two away, Steve, and here's Rodney Hammond, who struck out last time against Richter. This time, he swings at the first pitch and bounces a two-hopper down to Kevin Finley at third. Kevin snares it and fires across to first baseman Denny Hill to retire the side. The Blue Sox still lead the Barons, 3-2."

*The Blue Sox fail to add insurance runs in the eighth, but they don't need any. Ron Richter mows the Barons down in order in the ninth.*

BLUE SOX WIN!

"Here's the pitch . . . and the Kid lays down a beauty of a bunt to the first-base side! Catcher Buzz Saw Bradshaw has to field it. He throws to first . . . but not in time! The Kid is safe and Rusty Mills moves to second."

"That was a good bunt situation, Tim. The Kid bunted to the right spot, with Rhodes being a lefty and the first baseman holding the runner."

"Here comes Hector Peña to bat, Steve. Rhodes throws . . . and it's a line single to right centerfield! Rusty Mills is going to score! Here comes Ace Edwards's throw . . . Rusty slides . . . and he's safe! The Kid moves to third. We've got a tie game!"

"Good play by the Kid, taking that extra base on the throw home, Tim."

"The next batter is Kevin Finley, Steve. He swings . . . and lifts a fly ball to centerfield. The Kid is on third, ready to run as soon as Herm Davis catches the ball. Davis has it. There goes the Kid . . . here comes the throw . . . he's safe! The ball game is over! Great heads-up play by the Kid to help win this one, 5-4."

BLUE SOX WIN!

71

"Hub King is going to stay in the game, Tim, but the Blue Sox have a new catcher. The Kid is in for Cal Scott."

"That's right, Steve. And coming up to bat for the Barons is Herm Davis. Hub's first pitch is . . . lined to the opposite field for a base hit! Rightfielder Stroke Thurman was playing Davis to pull and now must chase the ball as it rolls into the corner. Ace Edwards scores to tie the game, and Davis cruises into third. Vince Rizzo is the next batter . . . and he hits a rocket, deep to leftfield! It might be . . . it could be . . . it is! A home run! Two runs score, and the Barons take a 5-3 lead."

"And that will be all for Hub King, Tim. Ron Richter is coming in to put out the fire."

*And he does. Neither team scores through the middle of the eighth inning, when the Blue Sox come to bat, still trailing the Barons, 5-3.*

"The Blue Sox are trying to start a rally, Steve. Speedy Green is on first base with a leadoff single, and Denny Hill is batting with a 2-0 count. We may see some fireworks here."

| Inning: 8 | At Bat: Blue Sox |
| --- | --- |
| Score: Barons 5, Blue Sox 3 | |

| Batter | Balls | Strikes | Outs |
| --- | --- | --- | --- |
| Hill, 1B | 2 | 0 | 0 |

Ken Rhodes isn't giving up any cheap hits, so you have to make the most of your opportunities.

You have Speedy on first, no outs, and Denny is ahead in the count. Maybe you should have Speedy steal second. He's not the tying or go-ahead run, but he would move into scoring position. Denny would have to let this pitch go without swinging at it, though.

Or, you could try a hit-and-run play. Speedy would run on the pitch, but Denny would try to hit the ball on the ground. A base hit could lead to a big inning. But a line drive could be caught and turned into a double play.

Grampa's in the clubhouse, looking through old yearbooks. It's your move, Kid.

THE KID

- To have Speedy try to steal, turn to page 74.
- To play hit-and-run, turn to page 90.

"Ken Rhodes sets. Here's the pitch . . . and there goes Speedy Green! He's trying to steal second. Catcher Buzz Saw Bradshaw throws . . . Speedy slides . . . and he's safe!"

"That's stolen base number 20 for Speedy, Tim, and the Blue Sox have a runner in scoring position."

"That pitch was called a strike, Steve. Here's Rhodes's 2-1 delivery . . . and Denny Hill hits it deep to rightfield. Ace Edwards is going to catch this one. Speedy tags up at second, and he'll cruise into third. One out, and the batter is Stroke Thurman, who also hits a fly ball — this one to centerfield. Herm Davis will get this with no problem. Speedy tags up again. He's trying to score! Here comes Davis's two-hop throw to the plate . . . not in time! Rusty Mills flies out to center to end the inning, but the Blue Sox scratch out a run. The Barons now lead, 5-4."

*The game moves to the top of the ninth.*

"The Barons are threatening to add to their lead. Buzz Saw Bradshaw is on second base with a double, there's one out, and Ace Edwards, a clever lefthanded hitter, is coming up."

74

| Batter | Balls | Strikes | Outs |
|--------|-------|---------|------|
| Edwards, RF | 0 | 0 | 1 |

**THE KID**

Ace Edwards can hit with control and with power. In other words, he's dangerous. Now that you have pulled within a run, it would be a shame to let the Barons score again. Maybe it's time to think about a pitching change.

How about Alan Sorensen? Grampa usually likes to use him only when we're ahead in the ninth inning, but Alan has a sizzling fastball that could get us out of this jam. Then again, Ron Richter has done pretty well so far by just picking away at the strike zone. Can he keep it up? Edwards is stepping in. Time to decide.

- To keep Ron Richter in, turn to page 81.
- To bring in Alan Sorensen, turn to page 76.

"Ace Edwards can hit just about anything and hit it with power, Tim. The Blue Sox need someone who can overpower him. And here comes Alan Sorensen into the game."

"Thanks, Steve. Alan finishes his warm-ups, and Edwards steps into the batter's box. Strike one . . . strike two . . . strike three! Now there are two outs."

"Whew! Big swings by Edwards, Tim, but he wasn't anywhere close to the ball. Alan's fastball really took off."

"Here's Herm Davis stepping in . . . strike one . . . strike two . . . strike three! And the side is retired. Alan Sorensen slams the door on the Barons here in the top of the ninth."

*The game moves to the bottom of the ninth.*

"The Blue Sox still trail, 5-4, and the Kid leads off. He swings at Rhodes's first pitch . . . and hits one deep to center! Herm Davis is on his horse, but he won't get this one! The ball lands at the base of the centerfield fence. Davis plays it back in, but the Kid is already on third with a triple. The tying run is on third, and Hector Peña is the batter."

"The Blue Sox have had a hard time hitting Rhodes today, Tim. Let's see what they try here."

| Batter | Balls | Strikes | Outs |
|--------|-------|---------|------|
| Pena, 2B | 0 | 0 | 0 |

Both Hector and Kevin Finley, the next batter, haven't had much luck hitting Rhodes today. Maybe you should force the tying run home with a squeeze play.

In a suicide squeeze, you run home the instant the ball leaves the pitcher's hand. Hector will have to bunt it no matter where it's thrown. It's a good way to score, but if Hector misses the bunt, you'll get tagged out.

**THE KID**

In a safety squeeze, Hector will only bunt a strike and you'll only run after the bunt hits the ground. You aren't as sure to score, but it isn't as much of a gamble.

The third baseman is holding you close to the bag. The crowd is going nuts, but you'll have to tune them out. You flash the sign to Hector.

- To try a suicide squeeze, turn to page 79.
- To try a safety squeeze, turn to page 60.

77

"Here's the windup . . . and the Kid squares to bunt. He lays down the bunt on the third-base side! Pitcher Ken Rhodes fields it quickly, throws to first . . . and the Kid is out! Rusty Mills moves over to second with one out."

"Score that as a sacrifice bunt, Tim, but I think the Kid could have gotten himself a base hit if he had bunted to the first-base side. You hate to give up an out this late in the game."

"That's true, Steve. Here's Hector Peña at the plate. With an open base at first, the Barons are going to walk Hector and pitch to the slumping Kevin Finley to set up the possible double play. Here's the pitch to Kevin. It's low . . . Kevin swings . . . and he hits a ground ball to shortstop Vince Rizzo. It's tailor-made for a double play. Rizzo flips to second baseman J.R. James, who pivots and fires to first baseman Walt Metcalf. The ballgame is over. The Barons hold on to win, 4-3."

## BARONS WIN

78

"Here's the pitch . . . and here comes the Kid! The suicide squeeze is on. Hector bunts the ball! Rhodes fields it, but the Kid slides across the plate safely! Rhodes hurries his throw to first . . . and it sails into the stands. Hector is awarded second base on the error. Tie game! Metropolitan Park is going crazy!"

"What a play, Tim! The Kid had a great jump from running on the pitch. And Hector did a good job bunting. The winning run is in scoring position!"

"Kevin Finley is the batter, Steve. Rhodes pitches . . . and Kevin hits a fly ball to deep center. Herm Davis makes the catch, but Hector tags up and moves to third. One out, and here comes pinch-hitter Mike Gilmore to bat for Alan Sorensen. Here's the pitch . . . and Mike hits a fly ball to rightfield! Ace Edwards makes the catch. Hector Peña tags up at third. Here comes Hector . . . here comes the throw . . . and it won't be in time. Hector scores! He's mobbed at the plate by his teammates! The Sox come from behind in the ninth to win it, 6-5. What a game!"

BLUE SOX WIN!

"Here's Ken Rhodes's 2-2 pitch to the Kid. The Kid swings . . . and belts a line drive! Oh, no! Vince Rizzo leaps and grabs the ball with the tip of his glove. What a catch by the Baron shortstop! And there's one out here in the bottom of the ninth.

"Tough luck for the Kid, Tim. He hit it hard, but Rizzo was in perfect position to make the play."

"Okay, Steve. Now Hector Peña steps in to hit. Rhodes pitches, and Hector lines a single down the leftfield line! Lonnie Snyder scoops it up and fires a throw in to second baseman J.R. James, holding Hector at first. Kevin Finley steps in . . . and he lines a single to center! Herm Davis has to chase it down, but he throws it back in quickly. Runners on first and third, and Mike Gilmore is pinch-hitting for pitcher Ron Richter. Rhodes pitches . . . Gilmore swings . . . and it's a hard ground ball, right at second baseman J.R. James! James flips to shortstop Vince Rizzo, who fires on to first . . . just in time to get Gilmore. Double play, and this ball game is over. The Barons win it, 3-2."

BARONS WIN

80

"Ron Richter stays in to pitch to Ace Edwards. Here's Ron's pitch . . . it's a curveball. Edwards times it perfectly and launches one, deep to right-field. That ball is way back there! It's going . . . going . . . gone! A home run for Ace Edwards. Two runs score, and the Barons take a 7-4 lead."

"It just goes to show you, Tim, that you can't monkey around with a smart hitter like Ace Edwards. A pitcher has to take it to him, overpower him, and that means fastballs — which Ron Richter doesn't have. That will be all for Ron. Here comes Alan Sorensen into the game in relief."

STEVE

"Alan finishes his warm-ups, Steve, and comes out firing. Herm Davis strikes out, and Vince Rizzo flies out to center, but the damage is done. The Blue Sox go to the bottom of the ninth, trailing the Barons by a score of 7-4."

TIM

*It's not the home team's day. The Sox go down in order in their final at-bat.*

## BARONS WIN

81

"Here comes the Kid in to coach third base, and there goes Ken Rhodes into his motion. Denny squares to bunt. Oh, it's a fake! Denny takes a full swing . . . and he lines one into right-field for a base hit! Ace Edwards runs the ball down, but he can't find anyone to throw to. Harold comes in to score! Speedy is rounding third, but the Kid holds him up."

"I don't know why the Kid stopped Speedy at third, Tim. With the rotation play on, Edwards didn't have a relay man. He took a long time before throwing that ball back to the infield."

"Well, Steve, let's see if Stroke Thurman or Rusty Mills can bring the run home. Rhodes throws . . . and Stroke hits a fly ball to short rightfield. Edwards makes the catch. Rusty flies to center, and the side is out. After three innings, the Blue Sox trail, 2-1."

*The Blue Sox tie the game on a home run by Kevin Finley in the bottom of the sixth. The game moves to the top of the seventh, tied at 2.*

"Only eight Blue Sox players have taken the field, Steve. Catcher Cal Scott is missing."

| Inning: 7 | | At Bat: Barons | |
| :-- | :-- | :-- | :-- |
| Score: Barons 2, Blue Sox 2 | | | |

| Batter | Balls | Strikes | Outs |
| :-- | :-- | :-- | :-- |
| Bradshaw, C | 0 | 0 | 1 |

**THE KID**

"Anyone seen Cal?"

Grampa Graff isn't kidding, Cal is missing!

"He's in here, Grampa," Mike Gilmore yells from the clubhouse. "But he's knocked out. He saw a guy juggling bats on TV. I guess he was practicing."

"Get your gear on, Kid. You're in."

Okay, you're behind the plate. Just when you get comfortable, J.R. James hits a one-out triple. Now, Buzz Saw Bradshaw hits a foul pop behind the plate that is drifting toward the stands.

Before you take off after the ball, you see J.R. James tagging up at third. The ball is going to land two rows back in the stands. You can lean over and catch the ball, but you'll be in a tough position to throw out James if he tries to score. What are you going to do?

- To let the ball drop, turn to page 84.
- To make the catch, turn to page 91.

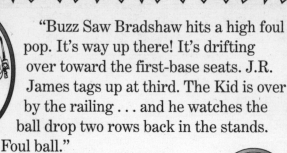

"Buzz Saw Bradshaw hits a high foul pop. It's way up there! It's drifting over toward the first-base seats. J.R. James tags up at third. The Kid is over by the railing . . . and he watches the ball drop two rows back in the stands. Foul ball."

"That was quick thinking by the Kid, Tim. He might have caught that ball, but he wouldn't have been in position to throw out James, who was ready to race home after the catch. Now, the Sox get another chance to get Bradshaw without James scoring."

"The next pitch, Steve, is grounded right back to Hub King. He holds James at third and fires to first. Two outs, and here's Walt Metcalf. Metcalf hits a fly ball to rightfield. Stroke Thurman catches it to retire the side, and James is stranded at third."

*The Blue Sox don't score in the seventh inning, and the game moves to the top of the eighth, still tied.*

"The Barons are threatening to take the lead here, Steve, thanks to a leadoff double by Herm Davis. Davis now moves to third on a wild pitch."

"Vince Rizzo is the batter, Tim. Let's see if the Blue Sox can dodge another bullet here."

| Batter | Balls | Strikes | Outs |
|--------|-------|---------|------|
| Rizzo, SS | 0 | 0 | 0 |

**THE KID**

This is a tough spot to be in. There's a runner on third with no outs. What are your choices? You can play the infield back in the usual position, let the runner score on a ground ball, and try to get out of the inning down only one run.

Or, you can have the infield play in, and try to throw the runner out if he attempts to score on a ground ball. The danger there is that it will be easier for the batter to hit one through the drawn-in infield for a single, and that could lead to a big inning. But this late in a tie game, it just might be worth the risk.

- To play the infield back, turn to page 94.
- To bring the infield in, turn to page 86.

85

"The Blue Sox are playing the infield in, Tim, trying to choke off the go-ahead run in this 2-2 ball game."

"Vince Rizzo digs in at the plate, Steve. Here's Hub King's pitch . . . and Rizzo hits a slow ground ball right at shortstop Speedy Green. Davis is going to try to score! Here's Speedy's throw . . . the slide . . . and he's out!"

"It looked like Davis was going to run on anything hit on the ground this late in the game, Tim. That play was close. Bringing the infield in saved a run there."

"One out, nobody on, and Rodney Hammond is the batter. He swings at the first pitch and flies out to center. Ken Rhodes strikes out to retire the side. The score remains: Barons 2, Blue Sox 2.

*The Blue Sox don't score in the bottom of the eighth and the game moves to the top of the ninth.*

"The Barons are threatening once again to break this tie, Steve. Leadoff hitter Lonnie Snyder has singled, and J.R. James is at bat, ahead in the count, 3-1."

"This is a big pitch for the Blue Sox, Tim. Let's see what the Kid calls for."

86

| Batter | Balls | Strikes | Outs |
|--------|-------|---------|------|
| James, 2B | 3 | 1 | 0 |

**THE KID**

With no outs, Buddy Phipps will try to get that runner into scoring position. He might have Snyder steal second or have James bunt him over.

Hub's next pitch must be a strike. But to make it hard to hit, it should be pitched to one of the four corners of the strike zone. It also should be in a spot where it would be easy for you to make the throw to second.

A pitch low and inside is easy to bunt and hard to throw. A pitch high and outside is best to throw but right where James likes to hit it. That leaves two choices: high and inside, which could be hit, and low and outside, which could be bunted. Each of them sets up good throws.

- To have Hub throw low and outside, turn to page 88.
- To have Hub throw high and inside, turn to page 93.

87

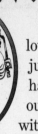

**TIM**

"Here's the pitch by Hub King. It's low and outside. James bunts! The Kid jumps out from behind the plate, bare-hands the ball, and fires to first for the out! Snyder moves down to second with one away. Steve?"

"The Blue Sox made the best of a bad situation there, Tim. They gave James a pitch he could bunt rather than one he could really wallop."

**STEVE**

"Buzz Saw Bradshaw steps up to bat . . . and Bradshaw lines a single to centerfield. Rusty Mills charges it . . . Snyder is rounding third and heading home. . . here's the throw . . . and he's . . . safe at the plate! The Barons take a one-run lead. Here's cleanup hitter Walt Metcalf, and he hits a two-hopper to shortstop Speedy Green. Speedy steps on second and fires to first. Double play! The side is out, but the Barons take the lead, 3-2."

*The game moves to the bottom of the ninth.*

"The Metropolitan Park faithful are rocking this old ballpark, Steve Daniels. The Blue Sox have the tying run at first with no outs, thanks to a leadoff single by Harold Carlson. Speedy Green is at the plate with a 1-0 count."

| Batter | Balls | Strikes | Outs |
|--------|-------|---------|------|
| Green, SS | 1 | 0 | 0 |

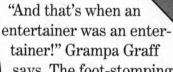

THE KID

"And that's when an entertainer was an entertainer!" Grampa Graff says. The foot-stomping of the crowd must have gotten to him. He's talking about a tap dancer he remembers from vaudeville. Once again, you're going to have to call the play. You've got to call it right. This is your last chance to win the game!

This might be a good time to have Harold steal second. He's one of the leading base-stealers in the league and could give us a runner in scoring position with nobody out. Then again, if catcher Buzz Saw Bradshaw throws him out at second, a crucial base runner is wasted. Maybe it would be better to play it safe.

- To play it safe, turn to page 92.
- To have Harold try to steal, turn to page 95.

89

**TIM**

"Here's the pitch from Ken Rhodes. Speedy Green is running . . . Denny Hill swings . . . and he lines a single to centerfield! Speedy rounds second and goes to third, and the Sox have runners on the corners with nobody out!"

"The hit-and-run worked perfectly there, Tim. With a 2-0 count, Rhodes had to come over the plate with a fastball, and Denny hit it right back up the middle. The Sox are down, 5-3, but they have a rally going."

"Stroke Thurman steps into the batter's box, Steve. He takes Rhodes's first pitch for a ball. There's another ball, and another ball — Rhodes is struggling. Here's the 3-0 pitch. He swings . . . and it's a high fly ball to deep rightfield! Ace Edwards goes back . . . he looks up . . . but you can kiss that baby goodbye! A three-run homer by Stroke, and the Sox take a 6-5 lead!"

"Here comes Buddy Phipps to the mound, Tim. And he's hopping mad. That will be all for Ken Rhodes."

*That's all for the Barons, too. Neither team scores for the rest of the game, and the Blue Sox win it, 6-5.*

**STEVE**

BLUE SOX WIN!

"Buzz Saw Bradshaw hits a major-league pop-up! It's in foul territory, drifting over toward the first-base stands. J.R. James is standing on the bag at third, ready to tag up if the ball is caught. The Kid races over to the stands, leans far over the railing, and makes the catch! Here comes James! The Kid can't get a throw off to Hub King, who's covering the plate. James scores easily, and the Barons take a 3-2 lead."

"Great catch by the Kid to pluck that ball out of the stands, but he had no chance to throw James out at the plate. It would have been better if he had let the ball drop. That way, James couldn't have scored and Hub would have had another shot at Bradshaw."

"Okay, Steve. Two out, and here's Walt Metcalf. Metcalf hits a fly ball to rightfield. Stroke Thurman catches it for the second out. Ace Edwards grounds to first to retire the side."

*That turns out to be a costly mistake for the Blue Sox. Neither team scores the rest of the way. And the final score is Barons 3, Blue Sox 2*

## BARONS WIN

91

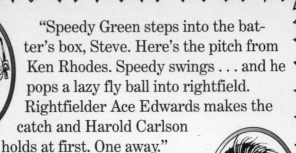

"Speedy Green steps into the batter's box, Steve. Here's the pitch from Ken Rhodes. Speedy swings . . . and he pops a lazy fly ball into rightfield. Rightfielder Ace Edwards makes the catch and Harold Carlson holds at first. One away."

"The Blue Sox batters have been having trouble putting two hits together against Rhodes, Tim."

"Here's Denny Hill in to hit for the Blue Sox, Steve. Rhodes's first pitch is popped up into centerfield. Herm Davis is under it, he's got it, and again Harold Carlson returns to first. Now, here's Stroke Thurman. Rhodes delivers . . . and it's another fly ball, this one to right center. Herm Davis is drifting back to the wall . . . and he's makes the catch. The ball game is over! The Blue Sox strand the tying run on first. The Barons win it, 3-2."

---

## BARONS WIN

"Here's the pitch . . . a high, tight one . . . James swings . . . and he hits a hard line drive to left that's going to drop in for a hit! Snyder is heading for third . . . James is rounding first! Leftfielder Harold Carlson plays it back to the infield, but not before Snyder scores and James cruises into second. The Barons take the lead."

"The Kid must have thought that Snyder was going to steal, Tim. Hub pitched one high and inside so the Kid could make a good throw to second. But it was right where James could spank it for an extra-base hit."

"Next up is Buzz Saw Bradshaw, Steve. Hub would like to escape without any more damage. But his second pitch to Bradshaw is hit deep to centerfield! Rusty Mills won't get to this one! James will score. Bradshaw is trying for a triple. Here's Rusty's throw . . . and Bradshaw is gunned down at third. Hub strikes out Metcalf and Edwards to retire the side. But the Barons now lead, 4-2."

*The Blue Sox can't get a rally going in the bottom of the ninth. They go down in order.*

## BARONS WIN

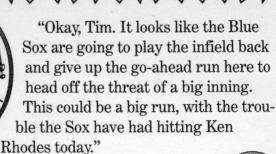

"Okay, Tim. It looks like the Blue Sox are going to play the infield back and give up the go-ahead run here to head off the threat of a big inning. This could be a big run, with the trouble the Sox have had hitting Ken Rhodes today."

"You're right, Steve. And here's Hub King's first pitch to Vince Rizzo. Rizzo hits a slow roller to shortstop. Speedy Green gloves it and throws to first to retire Rizzo. Herm Davis scores on the play. One down, and the Barons take a 3-2 lead."

"Ouch, that hurts, Tim. But Speedy had no chance to catch Davis on that grounder, not as deep as he was playing."

"Okay, Steve, and here's Rodney Hammond at the plate. Hammond swings at the first pitch and hits a fly ball to left. Leftfielder Harold Carlson ambles over and catches it for the out. Ken Rhodes strikes out, and we go to the bottom of the eighth. The Blue Sox now trail by one."

*The Sox don't score in the eighth or the ninth innings. The Barons win this one, 3-2.*

## BARONS WIN

"Ken Rhodes winds. There goes Harold Carlson! Speedy Green takes the pitch for a strike. Buzz Saw Bradshaw throws to second . . . but Harold is in there with a stolen base!"

"That steal couldn't have come at a better time, Tim. If you're trailing in the ninth, you've got to make something happen."

"Here's Rhodes's next pitch . . . and Speedy bounces a grounder through the infield for a hit! Harold scores, and Speedy holds at first. Tie game! Denny Hill is the batter . . . and he hits a hard single to rightfield! Speedy moves to second."

"Buddy Phipps has gone to the mound to talk to Ken Rhodes, Tim."

"Whatever Buddy said seems to have worked, Steve, as Rhodes strikes out Stroke Thurman. Now Rusty Mills comes up to a huge roar from the crowd. Here's the pitch . . . Rusty swings . . . and he drives one deep to center! It's over the head of Herm Davis . . . and rolling to the wall! Speedy Green is going to score! The game is over! The Blue Sox come from behind to win, 4-3! So long, everybody."

BLUE SOX WIN!

95